Mother, You're the Best!
(But Sister, You're a Pest!)

Diane deGroat

■ HARPERCOLLINS*PUBLISHERS*

Library of Congress Cataloging-in-Publication Data is available.
ISBN-10: 0-06-123899-6 (trade bdg.) — ISBN-13: 978-0-06-123899-4 (trade bdg.)
ISBN-10: 0-06-123900-3 (lib. bdg.) — ISBN-13: 978-0-06-123900-7 (lib. bdg.)

Typography by Jeanne L. Hogle   1 2 3 4 5 6 7 8 9 10   ❖   First Edition

Other Books About Gilbert

Last One in Is a Rotten Egg!
No More Pencils, No More Books, No More Teacher's Dirty Looks!
Brand-new Pencils, Brand-new Books
We Gather Together . . . Now Please Get Lost!
Good Night, Sleep Tight, Don't Let the Bedbugs Bite!
Liar, Liar, Pants on Fire
Happy Birthday to You, You Belong in a Zoo
Jingle Bells, Homework Smells
Roses Are Pink, Your Feet Really Stink
Trick or Treat, Smell My Feet

"What rhymes with 'mother'?" Gilbert asked. He was making a card for Mother's Day.

"Phooey!" Lewis shouted.

"That doesn't rhyme," Gilbert said.

"No," Lewis agreed, "but I think I just spelled something wrong."

Patty was more helpful. "How about 'brother'?" she said. "That rhymes."

Gilbert thought: Dear Mother. I'd rather have a brother. He sighed. His little sister, Lola, could really be a pest sometimes!

He finally wrote: *Roses are red. Violets are blue. You're the best mother, and I love you.* Then he signed his name and put x's under it.

Mrs. Byrd came over to help Lewis with his spelling. Lewis had written: *I love my mommy as much as salommy.*

"Hmmm," she said to Lewis. "Will you be doing something special for your mother, besides giving her a card?"

Lewis turned red and said, "We're going out to dinner. I have to dress up."

"I'm going to buy my mother flowers," Philip said.

Margaret said, "I'm going to bring my mother breakfast in bed."

Gilbert thought these were all good ideas. He wanted to do something special for *his* mother too.

When Gilbert woke up on Mother's Day, he tiptoed down to the kitchen to make breakfast for Mother. He put two slices of bread into the toaster, then poured some Wheaty Flakes, not just into a bowl, but all over the table.

Gilbert was putting the cereal back into the box when he smelled something burning.

The toast!

Gilbert scraped off the burnt toast, then put everything onto a tray, along with his Mother's Day card. When he picked up the tray, the orange juice spilled all over the card! He wiped it off as best he could and carried the tray up the stairs. Very slowly.

When Gilbert got to Mother's room, Lola was already there. Mother was reading a card that had scribbles all over it. "What a beautiful card, Lola," she said.

Gilbert didn't think the scribbly card was so beautiful. And when he placed the tray in front of Mother, Lola helped herself to a piece of toast!

Mother said, "What a wonderful Mother's Day surprise, Gilbert."

But Gilbert didn't think it was wonderful at all.

Gilbert went into his room and opened up his piggy bank. Maybe he had enough money to buy a gift. He counted out one dollar and four cents.

When he got downstairs, Lola was sitting in Mother's lap, holding a bunch of dandelions. Mother said, "Thank you for the pretty flowers, Lola."

Gilbert didn't think the weeds were so pretty. And he didn't want Lola to sit on Mother's lap. He asked, "Do you want to go to the store with me, Lola?"

Lola was excited. Gilbert had never asked her to go to the store with him before! She jumped right off Mother's lap and followed Gilbert to the corner store.

At the store, Gilbert saw many Mother's Day gifts—flowers, books, chocolate—but he didn't have enough money for any of them.

"I want ice cream!" Lola shouted.

"No, Lola," Gilbert said. "I want to buy something for Mother."

"Mother likes ice cream!" Lola said.

"Hmmm," Gilbert said. "Mother does like chocolate ice cream—and it only costs one dollar. . . ."

"I'll carry it," Lola said as they walked home.

"I'll carry it," Gilbert said.

But Lola started to cry, so Gilbert had to let her carry the ice-cream cone.

The sun was warm and Lola walked very, *very* slowly. The
ice cream started to melt. By the time they got home, there
was only a soggy cone left!

Now Gilbert had no gift for Mother, and no money. Just a
little sister covered with chocolate ice cream!

Gilbert didn't want Mother to see the mess. "You need a bath," he said. Lola was excited. Gilbert had never given her a bath before! She hopped right out of her dirty clothes and into the bathtub.

But Gilbert had to play rubber ducky races before Lola would let him wash the ice cream out of her hair.

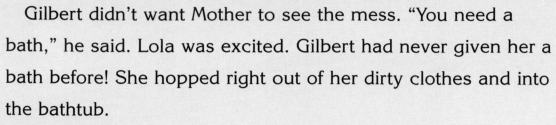

After lunch, Mother wanted to take a nap in the hammock. Lola climbed into the hammock with her.

Gilbert didn't want Lola to snuggle with Mother. He said, "You can nap in your own bed, Lola. Come on—I'll read you a story."

Lola was excited. Gilbert had never wanted to help with naptime before! She jumped right out of the hammock and ran up to her room.

Gilbert started to read a story about a Martian spaceman,
but Lola cried until he read her favorite book, *Goodnight Moon*.
Three times.

When Lola was finally asleep, Gilbert went outside to be with Mother, but she wasn't there. He sat down on the steps and sighed. Just then Mother came outside and sat down next to him. She opened up a photo album. On the first page was a picture of a baby possum, crying.

Gilbert made a grumpy face and said, "Lola!"

Mother laughed. "This is a picture of you, Gilbert. When you were little, you cried a lot, just like Lola."

Gilbert said, "No, I didn't!"

Mother smiled and said, "And you wanted to read the same story over and over."

Gilbert didn't remember that either. "What else?" he wanted to know.

Gilbert — 1 year

Mother picked Gilbert up and placed him on her lap.
She tickled him and said, "You wanted to sit on my lap
all the time."

Gilbert giggled. He still liked to sit on Mother's lap.

Mother said, "Thank you for taking care of Lola
today. That was a very special Mother's Day gift."

Gilbert was surprised and said, "It was?"

Mother kissed him on the nose and said, "It was just
what I wanted."

That evening everyone went out to dinner.
And for dessert? Chocolate ice cream!
It was just what Mother wanted.